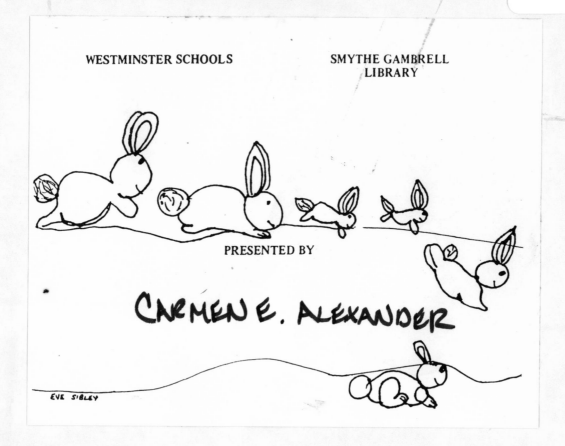

WESTMINSTER SCHOOLS   SMYTHE GAMBRELL
                                  LIBRARY

PRESENTED BY

CARMEN E. ALEXANDER

EVE SIBLEY

THE BURIED TREASURE

Retold by Djemma Bider · *Illustrated by Debby L. Carter*

DODD, MEAD & COMPANY · NEW YORK

Library of Congress Cataloging in Publication Data
Bider, Djemma.
    The buried treasure.

    Summary: Three brothers living in the Caucasus
Mountains discover the true meaning of their
father's claim that there is a treasure buried in
his garden.
    [1. Folklore — Caucasus]   I. Carter, Debby L.,
ill.   II. Title.
PZ8.1.B527Bu   398.2′1′09479 [E]   81-43216
ISBN 0-396-07991-1   AACR2

To Katie and Matthew.

— D.B.

For Grandma Carter and Grandpa Belknap,
two very wise gardeners.

— D.L.C.

Once upon a time, an old man lived in the Caucasus Mountains. He had a garden, and he worked in it all day long. He loved his garden very much.

His three sons loved the garden too. But they were lazy fellows and did not care for hard work. And hoeing, digging, planting, and carrying water is very hard work.

Still, each of the sons did do something now and then. The oldest went fishing. The middle son went hunting. And the youngest son took care of a neighbor's horses. But they did not bring much money home to their wives and children.

The years passed, and one day the father became too old to work. He called his sons to him and said, "Dear children, I will tell you a secret. I happen to know there is a treasure buried in my garden. You will inherit this garden after I die. If you keep digging in the earth, sooner or later you will find the treasure."

Not long after that the old man died. The sons grieved for their father. They buried him with great honor.

After a while they gathered their families, relatives, and friends together to discuss what should be done about the treasure.

"What if we have to dig up the entire garden before we find the treasure?" the oldest son said. "There is no way we can guess where it lies."

"Who knows how deep the treasure is buried? It will be such hard work," said the middle son.

The third son said, "What you say is true. Yet how wonderful it would be to find this treasure. We would never have to work again!"

They started to dream aloud . . .

They would trade some of the gold they found for money and buy wonderful things, and when they ran out of money, there would always be enough gold to trade again. All day long they could sit cross-legged in a tavern, chatting with friends, drinking strong tea, and smoking long pipes. What a life it would be!

So, they got down to work.

One morning while they were digging, their favorite uncle passed by. "Good day, my nephews," he said. "How is it coming along? I wish you good luck."

"It's hard going, dear Uncle," said the oldest. "And we certainly can use your good wishes. Who knows how long it will take us to find the treasure?"

"Indeed, who knows?" replied the uncle. "But since you are digging in the earth anyway, why don't you plant some seeds? Stop by my house and I will give you some."

The uncle gave the brothers plenty of seeds: pumpkin and melon seeds, cabbage and carrot seeds, parsley and pea seeds. And he gave them seeds for flowers: marigolds and morning glories, petunias and poppies, sweet williams and snapdragons.

And that was not all. He gave them saplings for apple, plum, apricot, and cherry trees, so that someday they could have an orchard.

The brothers did as their uncle had advised. They planted the seeds as they dug the soil. When they wanted to plant the saplings, they made especially deep holes. They watered the soil often.

Day after day they worked under the hot sun. Their muscles grew stronger and their skin became so tanned that their teeth and the whites of their eyes sparkled like the snow on the Caucasian mountaintops. At noontime their wives brought them goat's cheese, flat bread, sour milk, and cakes of rice and honey.

As time passed, the brothers began to love their work. They talked less and less about the treasure; often they forgot the reason they had started digging. The beautiful results of their months of labor began pushing and peeping through the earth.

At summer's end, the brothers had a fine harvest. They brought their vegetables and flowers to the market, and they were the best! Their watermelons were the reddest and ripest. How sweet were their Persian melons — they had a wonderful aroma. And what flowers their wives sold! Wealthy women, even those from faraway mountain villages, came to buy them.

Year after year, the brothers worked hard in spring and summer, and in autumn they reaped a rich crop. When the villagers celebrated harvest time, the merriest parties were always held at the homes of the three brothers.

And so the three brothers realized how wise their father had been. They understood what their father had meant when he said that sooner or later they would find a treasure in the earth.

Djemma Bider is the translator of HOW I HUNTED THE LITTLE FELLOWS by Boris Zhitkov, an ALA Notable Book and one of *School Library Journal's* Best Books 1979. She was born in Bessarabia of Russian parents and in her youth traveled extensively throughout Europe, studying in Paris. She has both written her own stories and translated the stories and poems of others, among them Chekhov and Nabokov, into English. She has also translated I.B. Singer and Saul Bellow into Russian. The mother of two grown daughters, she lives in New York City.

Debby L. Carter grew up mostly in Montreal, Canada. After receiving her B.A. from Mount Holyoke College, she returned to her native New York City to study art and illustration. She has written and illustrated her own book, CLIPPER. Her travels have taken her to Europe, South America, and Asia. She is married and divides her time between Connecticut and Manhattan.